Hold Tight, Bear!

RON MARIS

Delacorte Press

For some very nice people indeed

Published by Delacorte Press
Bantam Doubleday Dell Publishing Group, Inc.
666 Fifth Avenue, New York, New York 10103.

First published in Great Britain by Julia MacRae Books,
a division of Walker Books, Ltd.

The trademark Delacorte Press[R] is registered in the
U.S. Patent and Trademark Office.

Library of Congress Catalog Card Number: 88–18102

Manufactured in Italy
March 1989
10 9 8 7 6 5 4 3 2 1

Bear and Raggety,

Little Doll and Donkey,

are going for a picnic.

Over the fields,

across the stream,

to a meadow near the woods.

Donkey is drowsy.

Raggety is tired.

"Where are you going, Bear?"

Bear walks under the tall trees,

through the cool quiet woods.

"Is anybody there?"

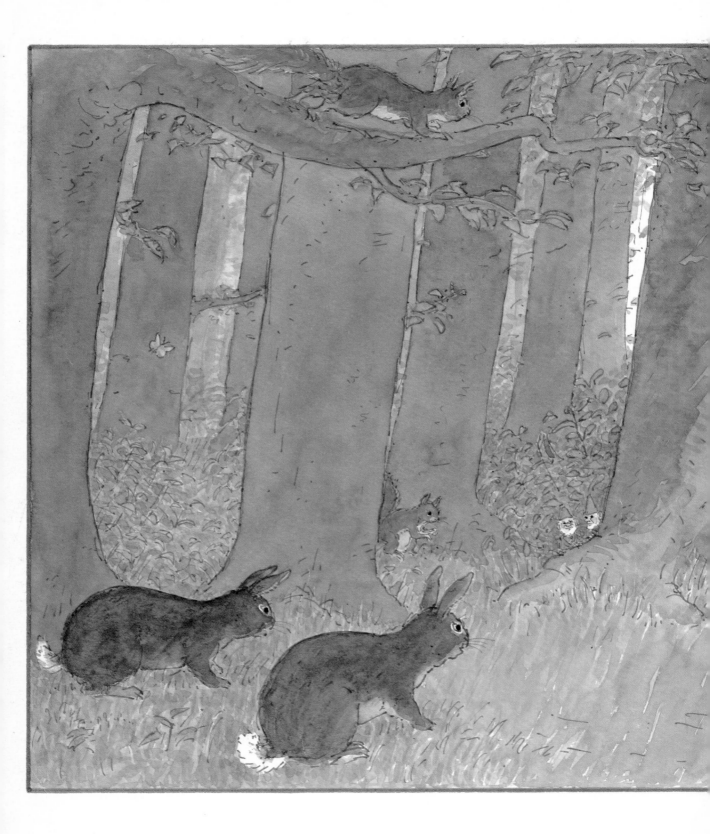

Over and over, and BUMP!!!

"There they are, still fast asleep."

"Wake up, lazy Donkey!"

"Follow me," says Robin.

"Through the wood," says Owl.

"How did you get down there, Bear?"

"We must pull Bear up," says Raggety.

"We can't reach down," says Owl.

"I know how!" says Little Doll.

"Wrap my sash round Donkey."

"Thank you all," says Bear.

"Home for tea," says Raggety.

"Shall I tell you again how very brave I was?" said Bear.

C

Hold Tight, Bear!

RON MARIS

Come for a picnic in the woods with
Bear and his friends — Raggety,
Little Doll and Donkey. See what
happens when Bear goes off by
himself! It's awfully nice to know
your friends will help you when you
get into trouble, and even better
to get safely home again with some
new friends as well.

Very young listeners and readers will
delight in the soft pictures and
the simple text about the adventures
of a most charming bear.